Seducing Her Boss
A FORBIDDEN FIRST TIME
TAKING HER INNOCENCE

CANDY QUINN

PATHFORGERS PUBLISHING

© 2023 Pathforgers Publishing

All Rights Reserved. This is a work of fiction. This book is intended for sale to Adult Audiences only. All characters depicted in this work of fiction are 18 years of age or older. All sexual activity is between non-blood related, consenting adults.

Contents

Preface v

Seducing Her Boss 1

Recommended For You 27
Free Exclusive Story 29
Become Candy Obsessed 33

Preface

Sign up to my newsletter to receive free, exclusive stories:
http://candyquinn.com/newsletter

Book Themes: Boss/secretary, bareback, breeding, virgin
Word Count: 5556

Seducing Her Boss

Being born beautiful came with certain advantages, but Linda knew how to take it those extra steps further. From the way she so expertly did her makeup and thick, lustrous blonde hair, to the skimpy little outfits she wore that exactly accentuated her full figure, her nipped waist, ample breasts and bubbly bottom, down to her long, shapely legs.

She'd been a model, a beauty pageant contender, but she'd put it aside for other ambitions. She'd worked her way up the corporate ladder to legitimately become the most prized analyst in her department, and that... got her to where she really wanted to be: In a private meeting with her tall, dashing, and--most importantly--rich boss, every morning.

Despite starting things off as a small business, he was now the kind of guy always in the magazines and over the internet, for his big business deals, as much as his daring jaunts around the globe, or in the sky. Handsome and muscular, he was in the gym every day, and it showed. He was also over twice her age, but that didn't bother her. He had that 'daddy' vibe all about him, even though he had no kids of his own.

Linda was gonna change that, she decided. Only problem was... he was a good guy. He never flirted or made a pass at her or anyone in the office, always respectful.

She approached his office in her high heels, just as he was getting back from the gym. His broad shoulders made him an imposing figure, especially at his 6'3 height.

"Hey Linda, just in time," he said, his voice smooth and charming. He opened the door for her, "After you," he said, as they headed inside his large, posh office, with it's windows overlooking the once sleepy street of their home town, which now--in large part thanks to the booming success of his company-- was a bustling community.

She wiggled in past him, brushing against him in a way that could seem innocent, but for her was anything but. She had to settle for the little things before she made her big play, and she knew that the soft scent of her perfume would fill his nostrils. The tight, a-line skirt showed off her perfectly round ass, and she leaned in towards his desk slightly, drawing her fingers down along to cup of her behind, as if she were smoothing out the strained fabric before she took a seat in the fine, leather chair he had for guests.

"I always do enjoy reading your mind," she smiled at him.

She knew without looking that she'd captured his gaze as she'd presented her backside like that, but the reflection in his windows confirmed it for her all the same. He paused, hesitated, then shut the door and entered in after her with a smile.

"You're good at it too," he remarked with a smile on his handsome, broad-jawed face as he rounded about the desk. "Want some water?" he asked as he poured up a glass for each of them before she could answer, then offered her one.

He wore his suit, with that sharp cut tie, and a shirt that clung to his hard, muscular physique underneath. But she knew he looked better without it. She saw some pictures online of him on vacation, diving to places usually only researchers went.

Yes, she was just a little bit obsessed.

She took the glass from him, that smile of hers never wavering.

"I bet the workout really built up your thirst, huh? I know after I get home from the gym, I'm practically begging for it," she paused, taking a sip. "Water, I mean."

Her eyes swept over him, lingering on his groin for a moment. And there she could see the outline of a sizable bulge. Either just his natural, resting heft, or he had a bit of growth there from the excitement of his workout. Or her.

He paused at her remark, then cracked a wry smile.

"Oh yes. You bet," he remarked after a delay, before downing some more water. He then went to the corner of his desk, and wet his lips. "So what's there to report today, Linda? Any new opportunities for growth I should be aware of?" he asked, placing one hand on his hip, which shoved back his blazer a bit further.

She laughed, her eyes twinkling at him from beneath her dark mascara. She kept her makeup light in the office, or at least to the untrained eye. But it all served to make her look gorgeous, even under the awful fluorescent lights.

"Oh, Mr. Rockwell, you know there's always opportunities for growth. I've done up my full assessment, of course, but the proposal I think you'd most benefit from is a bit…" she paused, biting down on her plush lower lip in thought, worrying upon it for a second. "Well, I just think that any report wouldn't do it justice." She leaned forward, sliding him the manilla folder that contained all of her professional thoughts and opinions, but it didn't contain the proposal she was talking about.

She opened it for him, the buttons on her white blouse straining against her large cleavage, and when she went to point at the cover sheet, one of them finally lost its battle, popping open and giving him an eyeful.

She pretended not to notice, instead talking about some of her more recent research into revenues and expenses.

As serious, respectful and work-focussed as Mr. Rockwell was, she caught him looking at her exposed cleavage. And then, after a few flits of his eyes weren't enough, practically staring at those pillowy mounds of breast flesh.

She could tell that her words were being mostly lost on him then, his hand in his pocket as he tried to focus on the report, but kept finding himself appreciating her stunningly beautiful body. Until finally he licked his lips, then cleared his throat. He forced on a casual smile again and nodded to her as she was partway through.

"You always know the market, better than people with several times your experience," he said, sitting on the edge of his desk and taking up the report, looking it over to figure out some of what he missed while he was staring at her more immediate assets.

"Mmm, beauty and the brains. The most dangerous combo, isn't it, Mr. Rockwell?" she asked, raising a brow. "I don't mind if you sneak a peek at my figures, you know. I could even show you what's behind them, if you had an evening free."

She could tell her innuendo wasn't lost on him, as his eyes went back to her, and a light flush touched his lightly stubbled cheeks.

"I, uh... I'm not sure it would be appropriate for me to meet with one of my employee's after work," he said, his voice losing some of that smooth, firm confidence. "Not that I wouldn't enjoy that, of course... " he added, just a tinge of awkwardness brought to this titan of men with her simple word play and a glimpse of her flesh.

"I hardly think you'd like me to quit, just to get a dinner with you," she said, looking up at him with her wide, mischievous eyes. "Or I could tell you about all of the inappropriate things I'd like to do and just have you fire me," she teased. "I could host you at my place, if it's discretion you're worried about. I'm a hell of a cook, to boot."

His eyes widened as her flirtations grew more bold, and he found himself licking his full lips once more. He reached up, tugging at his collar and tie a bit, as if the heat had risen in the room abruptly.

"A good cook too? You're a little too perfect, aren't you Linda?" he said, with what he hoped was a good natured smile. "I, uh... I would enjoy that a great deal, but, you understand... I don't want to make work awkward for you, or... or anyone," he remarked, putting down the file, his hand coming to grasp the edge of the desk right in front of her. That hand so big and strong as his bicep strained against his jacket.

She leaned towards him, looking up at him with an innocent smile.

"I do yoga, I promise you I've been in more awkward positions than this," she said before setting her glass down. "But I think what would be really awkward is if I leave this office right now and you have to deal with the big problem that's only going to get bigger if you ignore it."

As her hand began to withdraw from the glass, his fingers came to wrap around her wrist gingerly, but with that strength in his grasp apparent beneath the light touch.

"I'm used to handling problems on my own these days," he remarked, his voice dusky and low. "But... you have a way of bringing me problems and opportunities bigger than I'm used to, I guess," he said, squeezing her wrist, before relaxing that grasp. "You're a unique beauty, Linda..." he said, swallowing, his strong neck swelling.

"These things are only a problem if it's the boss putting pressure on his young, hot, available analyst. Not the other way around, Mr. Rockwell. I'm here to solve your problems, not create them. And you should never have to handle them alone."

He squeezed her wrist again, then... let it go. He stood up, and paced the room towards the window as he loosened his tie again, undoing the top button of his shirt, then peeled away his blazer. That thin white cotton shirt didn't do much to hide his hard, masculine figure, especially in the light of morning that streamed through the large windows.

She thought for a moment he might rally enough willpower to call it off, but then he turned towards her, mouth open, ready to talk, and... he swept his eyes over her figure. And she very elegantly, and casually, uncrossed, then crossed her legs, giving him a flash of her panty-less slit beneath that tight, short skirt.

Whatever he was gonna say was lost, and he drifted back towards the desk, standing in front of it, between her and it.

"Linda..." he said, that bulge now definitely having grown since he'd entered, thick and large before her eyes. "You can call me Malcolm," he said at last.

The corner of her lip quirked as she looked up at him.

"You don't like it when I call you Mr. Rockwell, Malcolm?" she asked, pulling her long hair behind her shoulders, making sure every inch of her cleavage was on display for him. "It feels a little naughty, doesn't it?"

He stared at all she had to offer, and she made sure he kept his gaze there as she reached up , to fondle that necklace she wore, the jeweled pendant of which was nestled between her two naturally large breasts.

"It does... when you conjure such... such inappropriate ideas in my mind," he said, swallowing again anxiously, then finding his hand reaching out, as if with a mind of its own. He didn't grab for her breasts, but he brushed the backs of his fingers along her blonde hair. "I haven't been with a woman since my ex-wife and I parted..." he confessed, licking his lips.

"That was years ago," she said with an empathetic frown. "You poor baby, I had no idea. I bet a night with me would let you really reach your peak performance. And I promise, if you want to go back to how things were yesterday, I can be a very good girl and not tell a single soul. But I think you prefer me just a little bad."

"You do always know what's best," he said vacantly, his breathing heavier as desire took over from his logical mind, and his thumb trailed along her jawline, down to her bottom lip. And then she felt his other hand reach down, resting upon her bare knee. "What if... what if I can't wait until tonight?" he asked, and she could see that thick, long outline of his cock had swollen up and was lewdly stretching through his dress pants in a way that anyone would notice right away, it was so prominent and huge.

"Then it's probably best to lock the door, Mr. Rockwell," she purred as she leaned in towards him, giddy with excitement. She never pushed so hard before, never wanted to play her hand too early, but seeing his response was like an elixir and she was drunk on lust.

He withdrew his hands from her body, then stood up straight. He ran a hand back over his sleek, short hair, took a deep breath then went to the door. His back was turned as she heard it click shut, but as his hand was still on the knob, she sensed the apprehension in him, his willpower waging with his desire. He didn't want to screw up, be the bad man.

"Linda... I... I'm being a fool, I shouldn't..." he trailed off, his broad, strong shoulders slumping just a bit, one palm pressing flat to the door. He still needed an extra bit of her charm.

"You've trusted me with your biggest deals," she said as she stood, sauntering towards him in her high heels. "You've let me help you in your darkest hours, and I've saved you more than once from making an awful mistake." She placed her hand on his hip, pressing her breasts to his back. Even with the heels, she was still almost a foot shorter than him, and so much more slender, despite her hourglass figure.

"If you were making a mistake with me, I'd be the first one to tell you and scold you for being so foolish. But fucking your horny analyst on your desk? I think most people would tell you not doing it would be far more foolish, Mr. Rockwell."

Pressed up against his back like that, she could feel the thrill in his pulse, how his mighty heart thudded loudly in his chest to pump more blood to his impressive cock. She could sense his raw masculinity stirred awake.

"I don't have any condoms," he finally said after a long delay with his internal battle raging inside his skull.

"I didn't imagine you would," she said with a lust filled purr. "I don't have any at my place either, and I wasn't planning on buying any. I wouldn't want to rob you of the sensation."

Her hand slid from his hip around to his front, teasingly close to touching upon his manhood through the thin cotton of his dress pants. He shuddered, that mighty mountain of a man trembling as he let loose a low, gruff moan.

"Linda…" he said, before slowly turning around to face her, looking down at her from his towering height. He grasped her by her arms, such a quaking fury of desire beneath his exterior. "I need you," he rumbled.

She beamed up at him, feeling the strength of that passion and excitement in him as her own heart raced faster.

"Sounds like you better take me before you burst,

Mr. Rockwell," she whispered. "I want to know every inch of you."

He lunged down then, his lips to hers as he kissed her passionately. He was more than twice her age, but he was strong, powerful, and ravenous for her. He slid his hands down from her hips to her ass, those fingers of his sinking into her supple ass flesh and inching up her skirt as he edged her towards his desk.

"Linda," he growled out, as her bottom bumped against his desk.

Nothing mattered, though. She was finally getting what she wanted, and she barely noticed that as she hopped up on the desk it tumbled the glass of water over the documents she gave him. She just grabbed his tie, tugging him towards her as her legs parted around his hips.

"I want you to show me what it's like," she purred excitedly, her lips finding his neck, licking and suckling him there.

His hands had shifted to her thighs, pushing her skirt up further as he kissed at her neck in return, peppering it with smacks of his lips, suckling lightly on that slender stalk. And then his hands moved to his waist, undoing the buckle of his belt.

"You're too good to be true," he rumbled, as his

pants peeled down, leaving just a thin layer of his boxer-briefs between her and that enormously large, throbbing cock of his.

"Do you mean that I'm better than you fantasized?" she asked as she shifted on his desk, pulling up her skirt so that it clung to her waist like a belt, revealing her shaved, glistening pussy as it left a mark on the fine wood.

He nodded his head, and pulled back enough to look over her bared, ready pussy. The sight of it causing such a lewd throb in his cock. That enormously long shaft of his was already beginning to burst out of his underwear, the purple crown peeking out as he stared at her loins.

"I always imagined you'd be so damn hot and good, but... but this..." he let one hand slide up her leg, his thumb caressing her inner thigh right next to her glistening slit. While the other wandered up, squeezing her supple breast through her top.

Her own hand went to his cock, coaxing it out of his boxer shorts as she stared at it with such fascination. She had a secret from him, and that was that she'd never been with any man before. She was a serious woman, and when she decided that he was the one she wanted, that was it. No other man could tempt her away from that.

So she looked upon the first cock she'd ever seen outside of videos, and felt it's heat against her palm.

It was fascinating to finally see--and feel--her first cock in person, but she had to admit... this one outdid even the pornos. It wasn't just that it was so long and thick, no. It was rippling with bulging veins, pulsating hotly with desire... desire for her. And that crown was so rigid and full, so well-contoured and it felt so damn hard it was probably stiffer than the desk she sat upon.

And her touch upon it, despite being soft and delicate, made him moan with desire.

"Linda," he rumbled again, kissing her neck, his hand squeezing her breast, and then beginning to pop open the buttons of her blouse, so he could reach inside and grasp that flesh bare, squeeze it, relish it's feel. "These are more than perfect," he husked.

She pushed her tits towards him, encouraging him to feel her skin as her nipple stiffened against his palm.

"I always wondered what it would feel like to have them sucked on. Do you like sucking?" she asked, her fingers still exploring his thick masculinity.

His deep eyes were lost in her as he pulled back, staring into her gaze before he began to lower himself down. It made it harder to grasp his cock, but luckily it was long and she managed to keep her hand upon it as he fell to one knee and parted her blouse open wide.

He shuts his eyes and leaned in, kissing around those two big, beautiful breasts, showering them with soft but increasingly passionate smacks of his lips. Until finally she felt his tongue trail around one areola, teasing it, before he wrapped his lips around it and granted her wish: he suckled and tongued that stiff nipple in his warm, moist mouth.

It was beyond what she could have imagined. It was so much more intense than just her hands alone, and the way he flicked his tongue over her nipple sent sparks down her spine. She'd never been more turned on in her life, and she could feel her sticky honey begin to pool on his desk.

"Oh God," she moaned, biting down on her lower lip as she began to stroke his cock with her fingertips.

Together they lost track of time, this giant of a man, both in size and stature, suckling at her ample breast, making her body course with such tingling sensations. He only broke off when the sound of his phone kicked in, alerting him to an urgent call.

But instead of taking it, he just switched to her other breast, luxuriating in the finest pair of tits to ever grace any bosses office. And she got to feel his pre-cum spurt out, and coat her delicate little fingers as he moaned against her tit.

"You look so good on your knees before me," she

purred, that pulsing between her thighs growing to nearly unbearable degrees. She couldn't believe that she was going to lose her virginity to her boss on his desk. Her wildest dreams couldn't compare to the reality, and she had no idea how much better he'd feel in real life.

He was slow to break off from suckling her breast one final time, his eyes opening and locking with her gaze. He pulled back, with a teasing tug of her sensitive teat, then licked at his lips as it snapped back, her ample breast jiggling with the motion.

"You're too much to resist," he said, before kissing the underside of her breast a final time, then pushing up, pressing her backwards as he seemed ready at last to mount atop her and claim her v-card. "I've jerked myself off to thoughts of having you here in this office so many times... but you were never as good in my mind as you are here in the flesh," he said, squeezing her thigh and breast to accentuate 'flesh'.

Her eyes sparkled at his confession, and she brought her fingers down between them. She touched herself, her wet pussy glistening as she gathered some of that honey up, offering it to his mouth.

"Look what you've done to me, Mr. Rockwell. I've made a mess."

"Let me help you then, you've helped me so many

times," he husked, before licking her fingers, then wrapping his lips around them, suckling away every trace of her glistening honey. And all the while he moaned with ravenous desire, that aroma of her pussy only exciting him more, causing his cock to throb and twitch enthusiastically, pulsating as he suckled at her digits.

She tugged him closer, using his cock like a lead, until finally his crown touched against her virginal slit and she let out a lewd moan.

"I have a secret. Promise not to be mad?"

His handsome face was enraptured, and he reached up, hastily tugging his shirt open, showing off his rippling hard chest, with a light sheen to it from his workout and shower. He nodded his head, moaning as his cock smeared pre-cum onto her slick labia, their bodily fluids mixing together.

"Anything... I'll promise you anything you want," he husked with such conviction.

"Good boy," she purred. "Because I need you," she said, letting the crown of his cock glide along her slick pussy, "to take my virginity. And you can feel dirty about it, but only if you let yourself feel real good about it too."

She watched his handsome face contort with the

shift in expressions. From raw, mindless lust to confusion, to surprise, to... guilt. And then back to shuddering desire as she continued to use his raw, hard cock to tease along her puffy, slick slit. He pulsated so thickly in her hand, spurting more pre onto her pussy as a full-body shiver took hold of him.

"I... oh god I shouldn't," he said, moaning as he half-heartedly tried to lift himself up to end things. Only to find himself shuddering with desire.

"You should," Linda purred, grinning wickedly at him. "This is everything I've ever wanted. I wouldn't trust my cherry to any other man. Only a boss can give me the firm, guiding hand I need."

"God Linda, on top of everything else... you're young enough to be my daughter," he groaned out, as his hips began to act of their own accord, and she felt that thick, raw hard cock begin to push down into her, making her little pussy canal stretch around the head of his manhood as he gave a long, low moan.

She moaned with him, her witty retorts and teasing paused by the sensation of him starting to enter her. Knowing how badly he felt about it, knowing how much he wanted to resist was just all the more reason for her to love it, and her tight pussy began to blossom for him.

"I want you so bad. I want to feel you fuck me. You wouldn't refuse your little girl her greatest desires, would you?"

"No," he said, shaking his head, slowly pushing that thick, hard cock up into her bit by bit, straining her little cunny to its utmost limits as he trembled and moaned. There he was, one of the richest, most powerful men in her part of the world, and she'd brought him to heel with only her words, and her beautiful, perfectly cared for body.

And then... the feeling of her slick canal wrapped around his thick, veiny cock overcame his last resistances. Because he shoved his dick up into her with one smooth, hard thrust, hilting himself inside her as he threw back his head and moaned.

It was ecstasy. She leaned back on the desk, pushing everything out of the way so that she could feel him sink into her. Her legs wrapped around his back as she lay back, her world spinning as her boss took her innocence, and let her feel that perfect cock as it pulsed inside her.

He shuddered over her, his bulging pecs and rippling abs tensed up as he looked over her beautiful body, seeing her bare tits jiggle atop her chest as she lay back and shoved everything out of the way. He muttered to her in a weak promise that even he didn't believe, "I'll... I'll pull out before I cum," he said, as he tugged back his hips and then thrust into her again, beginning to fuck her as he moaned and gasped, pumping into her with a rising pace as one of his hands held him up and the other gripped her thigh tightly.

"And waste your most virile load?" she chastised breathily, her body writhing against him. "Why would you do that, Mr. Rockwell? I want the full experience."

He gripped her tighter, locking eyes with her at those words as he rewarded her with even harder thrusts. Those pounding pumps of his hips causing her body to jarringly shake, her tits to jiggle, and he ate up that delicious sight, moaning all the while.

"You want it all... you tempting vixen," he half-growled out. "Fuck! You feel so damn good," he said, his eyes rolling back into his head as he hammered into her fast and hard, picking up his pace so that his desk shook beneath them. "How can it feel this good...?" he moaned out.

She moaned in response, her grin almost drunken in excitement and desire.

"I've wanted you for so long. You're just lucky I had so much self control. But then I decided that I actually like taking a risk when it's with you."

She had this stunning, adonis of a man wrapped

around her little... pussy. And he gave her exactly what she dreamt of and more, as he pounded into her, fast and hard, with a ravenous male desire to have her, to possess her. To claim her and sew his seed in her.

Mr. Rockwell grunted and moaned, his body quaking as his balls slapped against her bare ass. If the office wasn't completely sound proof, someone was bound to hear something, as the crashing of their bodies together resonated loudly, each slap filling the air, his moans and her cries resounding.

"Fuck! Fuck your tight little pussy feels better than anything," he groaned out, his hand moving to her breast, to squeeze and play with it.

"We were meant to be together," she moaned in return, her back arching to thrust her tit closer to him. "God, I was made for you. You're so fucking hot!"

He squeezed her breast tighter, his dick throbbing inside her, growing thicker as he moaned out loudly.

"I'm gonna cum soon...!" he cried out in a choked breath. "Oh fuck... fuck I need you, Linda," he panted out, spurting more pre-cum into her as his body was lit afire by the intensity of his pleasure. All those rippling hard muscles tensing up, bulging, glistening with a thin sheen of perspiration.

Her legs tightened around his hips, drawing him in closer and not letting him thrust out so far at his declaration. She didn't want him to find some shred of control and pull out, not when she was so close to cumming all over his dick.

"Tell me how much you need me," she breathed out. "Tell me, and I'll let you knock me up, and I'll cum so hard on you that you'll almost pass out."

He grunted and moaned, his body quaking even as it so powerfully hammered into her, making her body explode with new sensations. He gasped and struggled to speak again as his balls tightened.

"I need you... need you so bad," he began, his brain refusing to string words together, it was such a struggle. "I'd give anything... everything I have to know I can keep fucking you. Please... please let me knock you up and I'll give you anything you ask for!" he cried out, his cock throbbing so thickly, he was now struggling to hold back his release.

He promised her the world, and her legs tightened around him, pulling him in so deep as she arched her hips towards him.

"Good boy, Mr. Rockwell," she panted out, but no matter how cocky she was trying to seem, she couldn't hold back a second longer. It was all so perfect, so good, and her body was so sensitive that every thrust was a tortuous delight. Her pussy tightened around him as her muscles tensed, her body begging for his virile cum.

And she got exactly what she wanted.

Mr. Rockwell threw back his head, squeezed her breast and let loose such a roar of pleasure as his cock erupted. That enormous shaft shooting thick strands of his seed deep inside her, flooding her depths, filling her womb and then some. He was, just as he said, backed up. Years without the release of a woman's satisfying pussy, had meant he had so much seed to flood her with, to put towards sewing his child inside her.

"L-Linda!" he choked out, grinding his hips into her, shoving that cock deep up into her depths as he unloaded every last strand of his semen.

She was speechless as his orgasm sent off another intense wave of aftershocks through her, making her head spin as her pussy milked him of every last drop of his cum. It was the most amazing feeling in the world, and she knew that she was going to be addicted to him from that moment on.

He thrust into her a few final times, as she was overwrought with her own orgasm, and him with his. Until they were both so utterly spent, and he fell upon her, showering her with kisses, caresses, and a muttered, "I'm a bad man... you were just too good to resist."

Linda was on time for their morning meeting, same as ever. Her skirt and blouse perfectly poised, her high heels clicking, a smile on her pouty lips. She met Mr. Rockwell at the door again, as usual, exchanging a, "Good morning," with each other before heading on inside as he held the door open.

"I have been so anxious about this morning's meeting," he said to her, before she went to her seat, and he shut the door after them. The lock clicking shut.

"Why's that, Mr. Rockwell?" she asked, crossing her legs daintily.

"Well... I wasn't sure if... you know," he remarked, coming around to stand before her, leaning back against his desk as his eyes swept over her, hungry with lust.

"If I'd be up for more fun?" she said, a devious little grin tugging at the corner of her lips.

"Yes. You know... considering your--" he began.

"My condition," she said, finishing for him.

"Right," he said, smiling sheepishly.

"Don't worry," she said, her hands coming up to

cradle her very pregnant belly, caressing the smooth roundness of it. "I wouldn't dare leave the president of the company, and my co-owner, pent up and distracted on another important business day," she said with a ravenous glint in her eye.

Subscribe for more Candy Quinn:
http://candyquinn.com/newsletter

Recommended For You

For a full list of all my books, or to browse by length or kink, please visit my website!

https://candyquinn.com/books

YOUR NEXT HOT READ

Claimed by My Fiancé's Dad

Claimed by my Best Friend's Dad

Stripping for my Boyfriend's Dad

Off Limits Neighbor

Temptation Island

Free Exclusive Story
LUST LESSONS: BELLA

She has the hots for teacher

Mr. Wright is totally off limits. Not only is he her teacher, but he's also her brother's best friend.

Bella has never wanted anyone more. At first, she just wants to tease him. She doesn't wear panties, and practically begs him for the big D —- detention — just to prove to him how good she is at being bad. But he wants more than a tease. He wants to claim her fertile, innocent body, and neither of them can resist their forbidden desires.

TEASER

By the time the bell rang and the other students rushed out, Bella's fantasies had her wound up tighter than a knot. Her bare pussy was dripping on her chair, and she slipped out of it eagerly.

"Well, Mr. Wright, you got me alone," she grinned.

Clark gave her a cautionary look, before he went to the door and shut it tight then locked it.

"You really chose an... interesting way to get yourself in trouble, Bella," he said to her as he returned from the door, shaking his head at her in surprised disbelief, a soft chuckle escaping his lips. "But you always were a little terror of a tease," he said as he made his way back towards the class windows, beginning to slide the curtains shut.

"You make it sound so sweet," she giggled, sitting on his desk. She pulled her white skirt out from under her, crossing her legs as she watched him shut the curtains. "I just did what felt natural."

FREE EXCLUSIVE STORY

Get your free copy of Lust Lessons: Bella, and so much more! All you have to do is subscribe to my newsletter.
http://candyquinn.com/newsletter

Become Candy Obsessed

For over a decade, I've been writing the hottest, naughtiest stories I can think of, and I'm addicted. I love to explore the forbidden, the taboo, and the over-the-top sexy. Each story starts off with a sizzle, giving you that nice build up, and that perfect release.

Discover new, secret fantasies, or just indulge in those sticky-sweet guilty pleasures. I'll never judge! Make sure to follow me on your fave site so you never miss a new release.

Plus, if you **sign up for my mailing list**, you'll get updates on my new books, bundles, giveaways, and several **free, exclusive books.**

Connect with Candy!
candyquinn.com
candyquinn.com/newsletter
candy.quinn.erotica@gmail.com

Follow me Everywhere!

- facebook.com/candyquinnromance
- twitter.com/sexycandyquinn
- amazon.com/Candy-Quinn/e/B00K187NCE
- bookbub.com/authors/candy-quinn

© 2023 Pathforgers Publishing

First published in 2021

All Rights Reserved. No part of this publication may be reproduced, distributed, or transmitted in any form or by any means. If you downloaded an illegal copy of this book and enjoyed it, please buy a legal copy.

This is a work of fiction. Names, characters, business, events and incidents are the products of the author's imagination. Any resemblance to actual persons, living or dead, or actual events is purely coincidental.

This book is intended for sale to Adult Audiences only. All sexually active characters in this work are over 18. All sexual activity is between non-blood related, consenting adults.

Cover Design: Pathforgers Publishing. All cover art makes use of stock photography and all persons depicted are models.

Printed in Dunstable, United Kingdom